For Darrel

First US edition 2020
First published by Two Hoots, an imprint of Pan Macmillan (UK) 2019

Library of Congress Catalog Card Number pending
ISBN 978-1-5362-1659-2

WKT 25 24 23 22 21 20
10 9 8 7 6 5 4 3 2 1

Printed in Shenzhen, Guangdong, China

This book was typeset in Adobe Garamond Pro.
The illustrations were done in pencil and ink and rendered digitally.

Candlewick Press
99 Dover Street
Somerville, Massachusetts 02144

www.candlewick.com

Daisy Hirst

HAMISH
Takes the Train

CANDLEWICK PRESS

Hamish and Noreen liked to watch the trains.

"But where do they go?" asked Hamish.
"To the city," said Noreen.

"Oh, Noreen, don't you wish
we could go and see the city?"
asked Hamish.

"No," said Noreen.

"But don't you want
to ride in a train?"
asked Hamish.

"No," said Noreen.

"But if you think it's
so great, Hamish,
why don't you go?"

So Hamish went.

He followed the train tracks toward the station . . .

but when he got there, he found that he needed a ticket,
or money to buy one. So he followed the train tracks all day . . .

until it began to get dark.

Hamish had not found the city, but in a
railyard full of old trains and rusting junk
was a little caboose with lit-up windows
that reminded him of home.

"Hello?" he called. "Is anyone in?" Nobody answered.
Hamish put his ear to the door and heard a groan.
"Are you all right?" asked Hamish.

Inside, everything was made of something else—apart from Christov, who had the flu.

"I feel so heavy, so cold!" said Christov. "And I'm supposed to go to work in the morning. I work a crane on a construction site."

"Christov!" said Hamish. "Why don't I go for you? I'd love to work a crane!"

Hamish borrowed Christov's hat and jacket.
He used Christov's ticket to take the train to the city.

"When you get out of
the station," Christov had said,
"look up and you'll see my crane.
Then you'll know which way to go."

"Can't you read?" asked Max the foreman when Hamish explained he'd come to do Christov's job.

Hamish could read, and he looked at the sign.

He had Christov's hat and jacket, but Christov's boots
would have been too small.

Christov had given Hamish
some money for lunch.

It wasn't really enough for boots, but Margot gave him a deal.

"Right," said Max, "you'll need to
go on up there. Lisa's going to show
you the controls."

The crane was very tall.
"Taller than all the trees
in the woods," said Hamish.
"Country bear, are you?" asked Lisa.
"Yes," said Hamish. "But I really,
really want to work the crane."

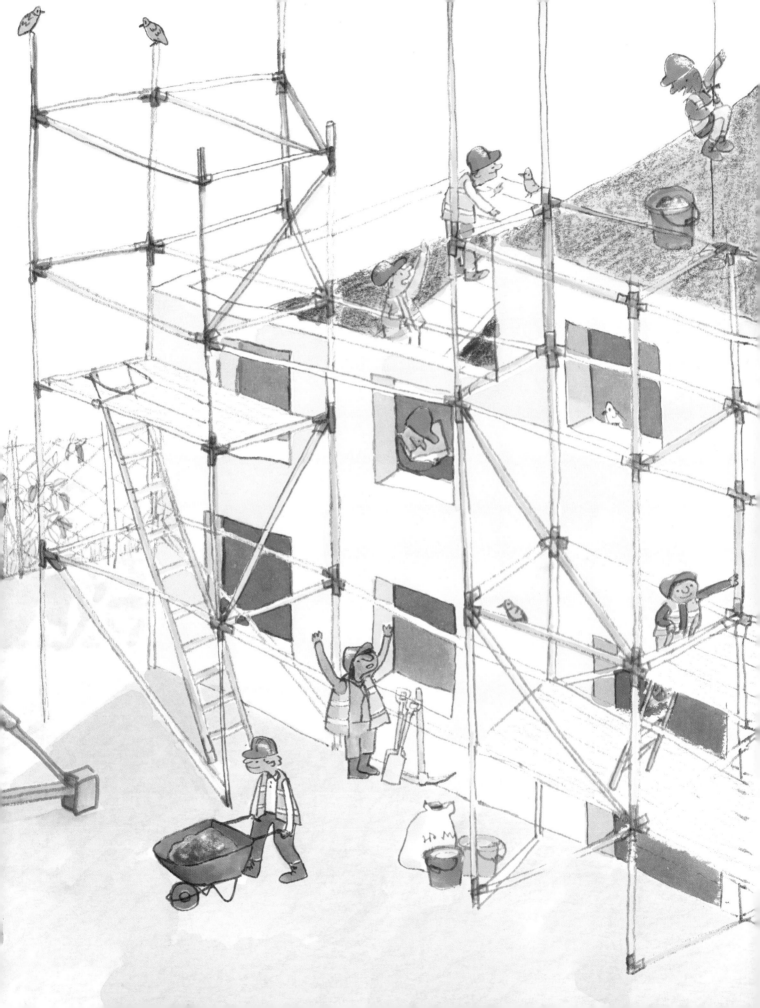

"Well, I
expect you're
very good
at climbing
trees,"
said Lisa.

"Quite good,"
said Hamish.
*But Noreen
is better,*
he thought.

It was cozy in the cabin.

Lisa showed Hamish the levers for moving the crane's arm and for lifting things up and putting them down.

Hamish worked the crane all day. The next day Christov was still ill, so Hamish went back and did it again.

From the top of
the crane, Hamish
could see the entire
city and the green and
blue beyond its edge.
He could even see the
curve of the earth.

On the fifth day, a
flock of Canada geese
flew past the crane.
Hamish found
himself shouting,
"Do you know Noreen?"

But the geese didn't answer.

Since it was Friday, Max paid Hamish his wages and said,
"There's a job for you if you want it."

Hamish bought a pizza with some of the money.
He wondered what Noreen would be having for dinner.

"So, Hamish, my friend," said Christov, who was feeling better. "What do you think of the city?"

"It's wonderful," said Hamish. "But . . ."
And he told Christov about Noreen.

"I miss somebody, too," said Christov, "but he's thousands of miles away. If I could reach him as fast as you could reach Noreen, Hamish, I'd go all the time! Nothing would stop me. You go and see Noreen."

So Hamish went in the morning, and this time he traveled by train.

Instead of walking all day, Hamish
found that, once he was on the train,

he was home almost at once,
running across the fields,
calling, "Noreen! Noreen,
I missed you!"

"Yes," said Noreen. "Yes,
Hamish, I did that, too!"

"So you're going to be a builder?" asked Noreen.

"Maybe," said Hamish. "And I could come home every weekend on the train. But Noreen . . .

you know when the trains come in the other direction, from the city to our station here?"

"Yes," said Noreen.

"Well, where do they go after that?"